Skateboard Star

Don't miss Catalina's other magical adventures!

Catalina Incognito
The New Friend Fix
Off-Key

BY JENNIFER TORRES

CATALINA INCOGNITO

Skateboard
Star

ILLUSTRATED BY
GLADYS JOSE

ALADDIN
New York London Toronto Sydney New Delhi

ALADDIN
An imprint of Simon & Schuster Children's Publishing Division
1230 Avenue of the Americas, New York, New York 10020
First Aladdin paperback edition November 2022
Text copyright © 2022 by Jennifer Torres
Illustrations copyright © 2022 by Gladys Jose
Also available in an Aladdin hardcover edition.
All rights reserved, including the right of reproduction in whole or in part in any form.
ALADDIN and related logo are registered trademarks of Simon & Schuster, Inc.
For information about special discounts for bulk purchases, please contact
Simon & Schuster Special Sales at 1-866-506-1949 or business@simonandschuster.com.
The Simon & Schuster Speakers Bureau can bring authors to your live event. For more
information or to book an event contact the Simon & Schuster Speakers Bureau
at 1-866-248-3049 or visit our website at www.simonspeakers.com.
Designed by Laura Lyn DiSiena
The illustrations for this book were rendered digitally.
The text of this book was set in Century Schoolbook.
Manufactured in the United States of America 1022 OFF
2 4 6 8 10 9 7 5 3 1
Library of Congress Cataloging-in-Publication Data
Names: Torres, Jennifer, 1980- author. | Jose, Gladys, illustrator.
Title: Skateboard star / by Jennifer Torres ; illustrated by Gladys Jose.
Description: First Aladdin paperback edition. | New York : Aladdin, 2022. |
Audience: Ages 6 to 9 | Summary: With the Valle Grande Skate Spectacular competition
coming up, Catalina is hoping her sister Coco will win and she can have her old board, but Coco
has lost her skateboarding mojo, so Catalina considers entering the competition herself.
Identifiers: LCCN 2022013592 (print) | LCCN 2022013593 (ebook) |
ISBN 9781534483132 (hc) | ISBN 9781534483125 (pbk) | ISBN 9781534483149 (ebook)
Subjects: CYAC: Skateboarding—Fiction. | Sisters—Fiction. | Competition (Psychology)—
Fiction. | LCGFT: Sports fiction. | Novels.
Classification: LCC PZ7.1.T65 Sk 2022 (print) | LCC PZ7.1.T65 (ebook) |
DDC [Fic]—dc23
LC record available at https://lccn.loc.gov/2022013592
LC ebook record available at https://lccn.loc.gov/2022013593

For Ava Mae, magical already

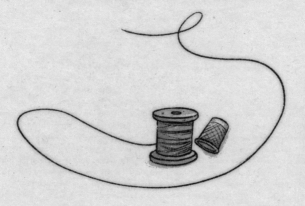

CONTENTS

· CHAPTER 1 ·

Skateboard Slump

I sharpen my colored pencils into perfect points and arrange them in rainbow order, just like I do every Saturday morning. That way, they are always ready when I need them.

I'm working at the kitchen table so that my baby brother, Carlos, who is rolling toy trucks on the floor with Papi, doesn't disturb me. You can't be too careful with Carlos around. I've found his tiny teeth marks on my school supplies before!

Right as I am about to place parakeet green next to lemon yellow, my big sister stomps past and bumps into my shoulder. She knocks my hand into the box of colored pencils and sends them tumbling to the floor.

"Coco!" I yell. She has never appreciated the importance of a good organization system. But that doesn't mean she can ruin mine. "Watch out!"

"Sorry, Cat," Coco says. She is carrying her skateboard and sets it down to help me pick up the pencils. At first, I try to keep them all in rainbow order. But then Carlos comes crawling toward us, drool dribbling off his bottom lip. I scramble to collect the rest of them as quickly as I can.

"What's the rush, Coco?" Papi asks as he scoops

Carlos back onto his lap. Mami won't be back from her shift at the nursing home until dinnertime.

Coco puts the candy-apple-red pencil next to the midnight-blue one, nowhere near where it belongs. "Can I go out skateboarding?" she asks.

She is already wearing her helmet and pads, and her old flannel shirt is balled up under her arm. It's going to be a wrinkled mess when she puts it on.

"Have you made your bed?" Papi asks.

"Of course!" Coco replies.

"Ha!" I bark.

Coco's idea of making the bed is piling her pajamas, sheets, and blanket on top of it in a lumpy heap. I should know. I have to share a room with her.

But Papi seems convinced. "Have fun," he says. "Be careful."

I take the red pencil out of the box and put it back where it's supposed to be—next to tangerine orange. "Wait up," I say. "Give me a minute to put the rest of these pencils away, and I'll come too."

Coco has been helping me learn to skateboard. Since all my chores are finished—including some that Mami and Papi didn't even think of—I can go with her to learn some new tricks.

"No!" Coco says.

"No?" I repeat. Coco doesn't always let me borrow her board, but she's never said I couldn't come with her to skate.

"I really need to concentrate this time," she says. "I need to be alone."

I turn to Papi. "Por favor. Pleeeeeeeease," I say, begging in two languages.

It doesn't work.

"Sorry, Kitty-Cat," Papi says. "Sounds like Coco needs her space."

Being called "Kitty-Cat" is pretty annoying. I've

asked my parents about a zillion times to start using my real name, Catalina. But even more annoying is not getting to go out with Coco. I grab the pencil box and storm upstairs to our room.

Not that I plan to stay there.

As soon as I hear Coco's skateboard rattle down the sidewalk, I go to my closet. I pick out my favorite sweatshirt. It's gray with kitten ears sewn onto the hood. My tía abuela—her name is Catalina Castañeda too—sewed it for me. Normally I wouldn't wear it. Like I keep telling my Mami and Papi, I'm getting too old for all the kitten stuff. But today the sweatshirt is exactly what I need.

I creep back down the stairs, tiptoe through the hall, and sneak out the side door.

Then, flattening myself against the house so that no one can see, I put on the sweatshirt. I zip it up to my chin. I pull the hood over my head. A shiver runs up my spine. I check my reflection in one of the windows. A gray cat blinks back at me. I am incognito.

Tía Abuela didn't make the sweatshirt with a regular needle and thread. She used a special sewing kit with the power to create magical disguises. Better yet, she passed the magic on to me!

I trot down the street to find Coco. She might have said I couldn't watch her skateboard, but she didn't say anything about a *cat* watching.

I find Coco at the end of the block. She must really not want anyone to see her.

I can understand why. She's wearing her flannel, but it's way too short, and her elbow pokes out of a hole in the sleeve. I shudder. I wouldn't want to be seen in that thing either.

Then again, Coco doesn't care very much about what anyone else thinks of her clothes. Something else must be bothering her. I step closer and stop to watch under the shade of a blue mailbox.

Coco tightens her helmet. She wipes her palms against her shorts and takes off.

I recognize this move. It's her signature trick, the Coco-kick. She steps down onto the back of the board and launches it into the air. Next she's supposed to flick the board with her toe so it spins underneath her. Instead she kicks it off to the side and lands on her knees.

Ouch.

She tries an easier trick, one she has landed millions of times. But she just keeps crashing.

"What's going on?" I ask. Only, I'm still incognito and it comes out like a curious purr. Coco lifts her head off the sidewalk where she's still sprawled.

"I was hoping nobody saw that," she said. "But you won't tell, will you?" She sits up and scoots closer to me. "You seem familiar. Have I seen you before?"

I skitter backward.

Coco shakes her head and unbuckles her helmet. "I need to land the Coco-kick for the Skate Spectacular," she says. "It has to be perfect. But I can't seem to get anything right. I might as well go home."

Home? Uh-oh.

• CHAPTER 2 •

Lucky Shirt

I race back home. If Coco were riding her skateboard, I'd have no chance of beating her there. Luckily for me, she's carrying the board as she trudges back, her face turned down to the sidewalk. I glance over my shoulder, and she's still two houses behind when I throw open the side door and race through the kitchen.

"Gato!" Carlos says, waving.

Oh no! I'm still wearing the magical disfraz, and

Carlos thinks I'm a cat! It's a good thing Papi is too busy warming noodles on the stove to notice.

"And what does a gato say?" he asks.

"Miau!" Carlos shouts.

I bound up the stairs, yanking off the sweatshirt. When I get to the bedroom, I grab a book off Coco's side of the floor, open it to a page in the middle, and dive onto my bed. I pretend to be deep in concentration when Coco walks in.

"Oh . . . hi!" I greet her, still a little out of breath. "How was . . . skateboarding?"

Coco grimaces. "What happened to you?"

"What do you mean?" I ask.

She points. "Your face. Your hair. Your *shoes*."

I touch my cheek—warm and sweaty. I pat my hair—curls tangled. I glance down at my feet— shoes still on, even though I'm on the bed. Usually I am perfectly put together.

"I guess I got carried away with the story," I fib. "I just got to a really good part."

Coco tilts her head and squints at the book cover. I turn it over and look too.

Amazing Math Puzzles.

It's one of the books Papi uses in the class he teaches at the community college. Whoops.

Coco tosses her flannel at me. "Well, if you're not too busy, do you think you can fix this?"

The shirt lands on my lap. Fixing it would mean I'd have to . . . touch it.

Coco's favorite flannel used to be a bright green-and-purple plaid. Now it's faded into a brownish-grayish color. Besides the hole in the elbow, it's missing two buttons, and the pocket is torn off on one side.

"Why don't you wear one of the new ones Mami bought you?" I ask. Mami has been trying for months to get Coco to replace her flannel. But the new ones just hang in her closet, unworn.

Coco flops down onto my bed, wrinkling the blanket. Now I'll have to make it all over again.

"You *know* why!" she says. She takes one of my stuffed animals and hugs it against her chest. "That is my lucky shirt. It's the one I was wearing when I landed my first trick."

I know the flannel is special to her, but it's time to retire it.

"What makes you think I can fix this?" I lift the tattered cloth with my pinkie.

"Tía Abuela gave you that sewing kit, didn't she?" Coco answers.

Coco doesn't know that the sewing kit is magical. I nod.

"And you've been going to all those sewing classes at the library, haven't you?"

Coco means Stitch and Share. Tía Abuela used to be a famous actress. Ever since she retired, she spends most of her time traveling the world. Since she wasn't going to be in town to teach me to sew, she made me promise to attend the weekly Stitch and Share sessions her best friend, Josefina the Librarian, hosts at the Valle Grande Central Library.

I haven't missed a single session. "The magic is only as strong as your stitches," Tía Abuela warned when she gave me the sewing kit for my birthday. If I was going to be in charge of such powerful magic, she wanted to be sure I had plenty of practice.

But I don't think Coco's grungy old flannel is what she had in mind. It's not what I have in mind either.

"Maybe your luck will jump onto one of the other shirts," I tell her.

Coco shakes her head. "There's not time to find out," she explains. "The Valle Grande Skate Spectacular is coming up, and the first-place winner gets a new skateboard. I can't afford to take any chances."

"But you already have a skateboard," I say, trying to mask how much I wish *I* had a skateboard of my own.

Coco rolls over so she's staring at me. Her eyes glimmer. "Don't you get it?" she says. "If I get a new one, I can give my old one away."

I sit up straighter, almost bumping my head on the top bunk. "To me?" I ask. If I had my own skateboard, I'd never have to borrow from Coco again. I could ride it whenever I wanted to. In my mind, I'm already peeling off all those stickers she's plastered onto the bottom.

"Maybe," Coco replies. "But I can't give it to you if I don't win, and I can't win unless my lucky shirt gets fixed."

I pick up the flannel again. Maybe it's not so hideous after all.

CHAPTER 3

UNPREPARED

*A*fter school on Monday, I take Coco's flannel to the Stitch and Share session at the Valle Grande Central Library. During Stitch and Share, Josefina the Librarian opens the library community room so all the sewists—that's what Josefina calls us—can get together and work on our latest projects and practice our skills.

There are always plenty of people around to help if I run into any trouble. I'm sure the sewists will have great ideas for fixing Coco's flannel.

"Early as usual, Catalina," Josefina says when I push open the door and walk in. She is carrying a big plastic bin full of sewing supplies and scraps of fabric that people have donated to the library. We can take anything we need from the bin. When I first started coming to Stitch and Share, the bin was so full that Josefina couldn't get the lid to stay on. Now it's almost empty.

"Right on time to help set up," I reply. Punctuality is one of my specialties. Early for Josefina the Librarian is perfect timing for me. I start arranging the folding chairs in a circle. That way, all the sewists can talk and see what everyone else is working on.

Being the first to arrive also means I get to pick the one chair that doesn't have any dents or scratches or spilled paint from library art projects on it. I like my sewing station to be as perfectly put together as I am.

I settle in and open my sewing bag. I made it myself out of a pattern that was originally meant to be a pillowcase. It's made of a leopard-print fabric that Josefina picked out of the scrap bin for me.

"I thought it would be *purr-fect* for a fierce *cat* like you," she said. "Get it?"

Normally I would have reminded Josefina that I don't really like all that cat stuff as much as I used to when I was younger. But leopard print happens to be one of Tía Abuela's favorite patterns, so I made an exception.

I lift Coco's flannel out of the bag. I'd convinced her to let me wash it, promising that the luck wouldn't rinse out. The shirt is still faded. At least it smells a little better.

But as soon as the rest of the sewists arrive and

everyone else takes out their projects, mine seems dingier and dirtier than ever.

Piled on Señora Garcia's lap is a heap of shimmering blue satin and gold lace.

Mr. Hart has a piece of checkered wool that I can already tell is going to turn into a hat.

Even Anthony Becerra, the only other kid in the group, has brought something special. Anthony is in high school, and he's been working on dog and cat

toys to donate to the animal shelter as part of a service project. But today he takes out a whole dog bed!

I fold Coco's flannel into the tiniest possible bundle. I wish I had a disfraz so that no one would see me.

I have never felt so unprepared. It's an even worse feeling than falling off Coco's skateboard.

Josefina the Librarian claps. "Bueno!" she says. Good. "I see you're all ready for the Spring Sewing Showcase, and you didn't even need me to remind you. Looks like we are going to have some beautiful projects to share this year."

I raise my hand but don't wait for Josefina to call on me. "Sewing showcase?" I ask.

Josefina walks toward me. "How could I forget?" she replies. "This will be your first showcase, won't it, Catalina?"

I nod. It sounds very important.

"Well, every spring, we sewists put together a display of our work," Josefina explains. "We also collect donations from people who come see it, and use the money to buy new sewing supplies. This year

I'm hoping we can raise enough to buy a sewing machine for the library!"

Señora Garcia smooths the blue satin over her lap. "I'm making a gown for my niece's quinceañera," she says, smiling.

"Keen-seh-ahn-YEHR-uh?" Mr. Hart repeats the word slowly.

"It's a fifteenth-birthday party," I tell him.

Then Mrs. Glass shows us the tiny squares of fabric she's sewing together. "And I am trying out a new quilt pattern."

Josefina sits in the seat next to mine. "What have you brought to work on?"

I unfold Coco's flannel, wishing I had something better.

"I told my sister I would help her repair this," I say. "But don't worry. I'll think of something *way* better for the showcase." I want to help raise money for sewing supplies too.

Josefina takes the shirt and examines it. "You know," she says, "there are beautiful mending techniques that you could show off. Some people even make their repairs visible on purpose."

They *want* people to see what's wrong with their clothes? It seems impossible, but Josefina shows me pictures on her phone as proof.

Ms. Yoo pats her knee. "I sewed a patch onto these jeans, and I like them even better this way."

It's not that I don't believe them. But a showcase project has to be something special. Something surprising. Something *perfect*.

Coco's flannel is simply not going to cut it.

· CHAPTER 4 ·

Incognito

*H*ow am I going to fix Coco's flannel in time for the Skate Spectacular *and* sew up an amazing project for the showcase?

I hate to admit it, but I'm going to need help from Pablo Blanco.

Pablo is my best friend—and biggest rival—at Valle Grande Elementary School. No one else in third grade is as perfectly prepared as we are.

I plan my outfits a week in advance. Pablo brings

a spare change of clothes to school every day, socks and everything, just in case something spills at lunch.

I keep a color-coded calendar. Pablo schedules his weekends down to the minute.

He'll help me find a way to solve this problem. But when I explain Coco's skating slump, he says, "Don't you see? This is exactly like what happened in *The Kitchen Curse*!"

The other important thing to know about Pablo is that he is a major fan of telenovelas, the kind of super-dramatic TV shows that Tía Abuela used to star in before she retired.

I scrunch my nose. "Pablo, I don't think anyone put a *curse* on my sister—"

"Just listen," he says, interrupting me. He's so excited that he is standing on the tips of his toes. His white sneakers are spotless as usual. "What if one of the other skateboarders has *sabotaged* Coco, done something to spoil her chances so she can't win. That's what happened to Chef Marcela on last night's episode. Her jealous assistant, Salvador, cut the power to her oven right in the middle of the prince's banquet! Dinner was ruined!"

"Hmm," I say. I am not convinced that anyone is playing tricks on Coco. But just to be sure, Pablo

and I have agreed to meet at the skate park where she sometimes practices after school.

"To spy?" I ask Pablo.

"To *observe*," he says.

We crouch underneath a picnic table on a grassy hill above the park. We're a little far from the edge of the emptied-out pool where Coco and her friends are getting ready to skate. It's a good thing Pablo has brought his binoculars.

One by one, the skateboarders drop into the bowl. They gain speed as they sail down the smooth walls. Usually Coco flies out in front, swooping back and forth from one end of the pool to the other.

But this time, she hangs back. She twists the piece of hair that falls out from under her helmet. She doesn't even look like herself without her lucky flannel. It's

still hanging in my closet, waiting to be fixed.

Finally Coco rolls to the edge of the pool. She leans over and looks toward the bottom. Slowly she lets the board tip over, and she glides down.

"It's about time," I mutter. I wasn't sure she was *ever* going to drop in.

But then, before she's even reached the bottom, Coco jumps off and stumbles to a stop. The skateboard rolls away without her.

"Muy interesante," Pablo says, setting down his binoculars.

"*What's* interesting?" I ask. "Did you see anyone push her? Did someone mess with her skateboard?"

Pablo shakes his head. "No," he says. "It's that Coco is even worse off than I thought. Maybe you'd be able to see that for yourself if *you'd* come prepared." He glances at the binoculars.

"I'm going to get a closer look," I say with a huff as I

stand and shake the grass off my legs. "You stay here."

The truth is, I *did* come prepared. Prepared with something even better than binoculars. But I can't let Pablo see it.

I knew a disfraz might come in handy today. But I couldn't use my kitten hoodie. If Coco caught me in it again, she might get suspicious. Instead I set my alarm for extra early this morning so I could whip up a new disguise. It's in my backpack, folded inside a paper bag labeled *súpersecreto*, super secret.

I skip down the hill, darting from tree to tree so that Coco and her friends don't see me. When I get to the skate park entrance, I duck behind a vending machine. I unzip my backpack and remove my disfraz: a yellow pillowcase that I turned into a dress. I also sewed three black stripes across the middle so that when I slip it over my shoulders and step out from behind the vending machine, I am incognito. A bumblebee!

The other skateboarders scatter as I whiz by them.

"Look out, it's a bee!" one of them shouts.

Another swats at me. "Go away!"

I dodge and almost slip into the pool.

Coco doesn't flinch, though. She's never been afraid of bees. Then again, she's never been afraid of the staircase feature at the skate park either. Yet here she is, standing in front of it looking like she is too scared to go on.

I remember what she always tells me. "Just *try*," I say. It comes out like a buzz.

Then, almost as if she's heard me, Coco tightens her helmet. "You've got this," she tells herself.

"You do!" I buzz. Coco steps onto the board with one foot and pushes off with the other. She rolls toward the bottom step. I expect her to pop the skateboard up and to slide along its edge.

"Go, Coco!" But my cheer quickly turns into a cringe. Coco doesn't jump high enough, and instead of landing on top of the step, she crashes into it. The skateboard skids away in one direction while she stumbles in another.

"I don't know what's wrong with me," Coco says, rubbing her elbow. "I just can't do it anymore."

I gasp. Pablo was right! Someone *is* sabotaging Coco. But it's not one of the other skaters. It's *her*! Coco hasn't lost her luck. She's lost her *confidence*.

· CHAPTER 5 ·

A Surprise Package

*P*ablo waves his arms in frustration as we leave the park. "How can you be so sure the other skateboarders aren't behind this?" he asks. "I didn't see you anywhere near them, and I was looking." He pats his binoculars, which hang from a strap around his neck.

I can't tell Pablo the truth—that I actually *was* right next to Coco and the others. That would mean giving away the secret of the magic sewing kit. I shrug instead.

"Just a hunch," I say.

We split up at the corner. Pablo walks to his house, and I go to mine, the bumblebee disfraz tucked safely into my backpack.

I think about all the skateboard tricks Coco used to do. She was never afraid of trying out new jumps and twists. Maybe I can inspire her by attempting a big trick of my own—not with a skateboard but with a sewing needle.

As soon as I get home, I race to my desk and take out my notebook and colored pencils. (Luckily, they're still sharpened. It pays to be prepared.) Then I sketch out a new design. When I'm finished, I take it downstairs and ask Mami for help dialing Tía Abuela on video chat.

No matter where she's traveling, Tía Abuela always tries to pick up when I call.

I take the tablet to the couch in the living room and wait for her face to appear on the screen.

Bleeeeep.

Bleeeeep.

I'm not sure just where in the world Tía Abuela might be. Her travels are sometimes a mystery. Maybe it's too late for her to talk.

But then, right as I'm about to press the red button that ends the chat, she answers.

"Kitty-Cat? Is that you?" she says. "Qué sorpresa!" What a surprise.

A breeze is blowing Tía Abuela's silver hair off her face. Even though it looks like the sun is beginning to set, she wears cat-eye sunglasses with sparkling rhinestones in the corners. Just like always.

I catch a flash of red feathers in the trees behind her.

"Where are you?" I ask, leaning in closer to the screen.

"Belize, of course," she answers. "It's the best

time of year for bird-watching. I can't wait to show you my pictures. Qué pasa?" What's happening?

I tell Tía Abuela about the Sewing Showcase. How I want to impress the other sewists—and raise money for Stitch and Share.

Tía Abuela's cherry-red lips part in a dazzling smile. "I'm sure my comadre Josefina can help you come up with the perfect project." "Comadre" is what Tía Abuela calls Josefina the Librarian because they have been such good friends for such a long time.

But I don't need Josefina to help me think up a project.

"I already have an idea in mind," I say with a wink. "An *exciting* idea. But I need your help."

One of Tía Abuela's eyebrows lifts over the top of her sunglasses.

I hold my notebook up to the camera and unveil my sketch. "The Dragon Dress . . . two-point-oh."

The Dragon Dress is one of Tía Abuela's most famous costumes. It's a long, emerald gown, with gleaming red and orange gems at the neck. Tía Abuela sewed it herself, and it's on display in the Valle Grande library lobby. I can already picture my own, smaller version standing next to it.

"I think I have enough fabric left over from the box you sent me," I explain. "And I can use glitter from the library craft stash for the gems. But I'm not sure where to start."

I expect Tía Abuela to shout with excitement. I expect her to say, *Sí! Of course I'll help!* After all, she's the one who taught me my first stitch.

Instead she presses her lips together. "Remember,

Catalina, I sewed that dress after many years of practice. Don't be discouraged if you're not able to make it yet."

My shoulders fall. "Don't you think I can do it?"

Tía Abuela takes off her sunglasses. Her long eyelashes flutter as she blinks at me. "I know you can do it . . . someday," she says. "I also know that you don't need a dress to impress anyone. Your progress is what's most impressive. It reminds me of an old saying."

Tía Abuela has lots of old sayings.

"A camino largo, paso corto," she recites.

I can understand a little Spanish, but sometimes I need help. "What does that mean?"

"For a long journey, take small steps," Tía Abuela translates. "Learning to sew is a long journey. Be proud of the steps you have taken so far."

I try to hide my frown, but I can't. If you're on

a long journey, shouldn't you take *big* steps? To get where you're going faster?

"I'll send you a package," Tía Abuela says. "Something that will help."

That's exactly what I was hoping for. Maybe she'll send a dress pattern, or maybe some jewels to add to my design. I know better than to ask, though. Tía Abuela loves surprises.

Just then Coco bursts through the front door. I look up. She's carrying her skateboard. "You said you'd fix my flannel, Cat!" she says. "Are you finished yet? I really need it."

Mami glances up from the crossword she's working on while she waits for a pot of water to boil on the stove. "A promise is a promise, Kitty-Cat," she says.

I turn back to Tía Abuela. "Better go," I say.

Tía Abuela winks and says, "Adiós!"

· CHAPTER 6 ·

SEWING MAGIC

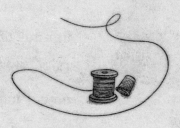

I'd rather start sewing my gown. But, like Mami said, I *did* promise. At least mending the flannel will give me extra practice while I wait for Tía Abuela's package to arrive.

There's also another good reason to work on the shirt: I still want Coco's old skateboard, and I won't get it unless she wins the Skate Spectacular.

I'm not sure fixing the flannel will help. But I don't know how else to get Coco's confidence back.

I march upstairs and open the door to my closet. I pull Coco's flannel off the hanger. Even though it's clean now, I keep it separate from the rest of my clothes. Like I said, you can't be too careful.

Next I gather my supplies and take them to my desk. I have collected a lot since I started sewing over the summer: thimbles and measuring tape from Tía Abuela, ribbons and thread from the sewists at Stitch and Share, and even a new pair of scissors that I bought with saved-up allowance money.

I keep all of it inside the practice sewing kit Tía Abuela left me. This one isn't magical. But it's *sort of* incognito. It's made out of an old tin of butter cookies!

Now that I'm properly prepared, I inspect the shirt, trying to figure out where to start. Replacing the missing buttons will be easiest, I decide.

I open the cookie tin and push supplies around until my fingers land on two spare buttons. A red one I snipped off a shirt that doesn't fit anymore and a shiny gold one I found on the walk to school.

The buttons don't match, but I don't think Coco will mind. Just look at her cluttered closet or the stacks of crumpled paper on her desk. She might even like the shirt better this way.

When I first started sewing, it took me forever just to thread the needle. Now I finish sewing on the new buttons before Mami has even called me down for dinner.

The shirt is already looking much better. Like

it's not about to fall apart in my hands. I decide to move on to the pocket.

I snip some thread off a brown spool that's in the cookie tin. That will blend in with the fabric best. Maybe no one will even notice the tear.

Then I change my mind. I decide to follow Josefina's advice. Instead of trying to hide the repair, I will make it stand out.

"Orange," I say to myself as I choose a different spool.

For this repair, I use a stitch I've just learned: the backstitch. Josefina said it's very strong, which is exactly what Coco needs to keep this shirt in one piece.

When I'm done, there is a neat line of orange dashes along one side of the pocket. Perfect.

The shirt is looking so good now that a new idea pops into my mind. One I never expected. What if I *try on* Coco's flannel? I'm curious to know what's so special about it, and maybe wearing the shirt will help me fix it. I glance at the door to make sure it's shut. Coco will never even know.

Quickly I carry the shirt to my closet, where a mirror hangs on the back side of the door. I push my arms through the sleeves, first the right, then the left.

I tug it over my shoulders.

I straighten the collar.

I check my reflection.

It's a perfect fit!

I twist and turn in front of the mirror. Even though the flannel *is* old—and even though my elbow is poking through that hole in the sleeve—I don't want to take it off. I puff out my chest. I stick up my chin. Coco was right all along. Something about this shirt makes me feel stronger. Braver. *Luckier.*

That's when I realize something. Maybe I don't need Coco to win the Skate Spectacular in order for me to get my own skateboard. Maybe I can win it myself—with a little bit of sewing magic.

· CHAPTER 7 ·

SKATEBOARD STAR

I have to wait until it's Saturday again to test out my latest creation.

Coco lounges on the sofa, an arm and a leg hanging off the edge. Since I've already finished organizing my colored pencils, I am trying to show Carlos different ways to sort his blocks: by color, by shape, and by size. It's never too early to learn good organizational skills.

Carlos doesn't seem to agree, though. He throws

one of the blocks, and it lands on the pile of math tests Papi is grading. Papi sighs and rolls it back to Carlos.

"You're not going to go out skateboarding, Coco?" Papi asks.

Coco yawns. "What's the point?" she replies. "I'll never get out of this slump."

Papi scratches his forehead. "That doesn't sound like the Coco I know."

He's right. Coco hasn't even nagged me about her flannel lately. Which is a good thing, since I'm kind of hoping to keep it for myself.

"Well, you can't sit on the couch all day," Papi continues. "Why don't you take your brother for a walk in his wagon? He could use some fresh air. I have a feeling you *both* could."

Coco groans and rolls off the sofa. She puts on her shoes, then picks up Carlos and heads for the side door.

"You're not going with them, Kitty-Cat?" Papi asks.

"I want to, but I . . . umm . . . ," I sputter, trying to think up an excuse. "I have to finish something upstairs."

It's the truth. But only part of the truth. The flannel still needs one last touch, and with Coco out of the house, I finally have a chance to finish it.

I hurry upstairs before Papi can ask any more questions. Better get stitching.

This time, I don't use the cookie tin sewing kit. I reach for the other one. The *magic* one.

I keep it on the top shelf of my closet, and it doesn't look like anything special. It's an old pouch

made of red velvet, almost as worn-out as Coco's flannel. Inside is a brass thimble, a needle stuck into a strawberry-shaped pincushion, and a spool of silver thread—all the tools I need to sew a magical disguise.

Then I grab Coco's shirt and a patch I made out of a piece of black felt. It's shaped like a cat. It even has whiskers! Normally I wouldn't choose cat accessories *on purpose*, but I don't want anyone to mistake me for Coco when I'm wearing the disfraz. I want them to know it's me. Me, but better. A skateboard star.

I place the patch over the rip in the elbow and stitch it on with the silver thread. When I've gone all the way around, I tie a knot at the end to seal the magic.

The disfraz is ready. I put it on, and my spine tingles.

I am incognito. Kind of.

Coco and Carlos will be back soon, so I have to hurry. I race downstairs, out the door, and to the garage, where I find my helmet and Coco's skateboard.

I take a deep breath and roll out to the sidewalk.

Two of Coco's friends are across the street. When I see them, I put my foot down to stop the skateboard. They've laughed when I've fallen before. I'm not sure I can skate in front of them again. But it's the only way to know if the disfraz is working.

I step back onto the board and push off.

"You've gotten a lot better, Cat," Coco's friend Trish says when I get to the other side of the street.

"Yeah," her other friend, Albert, agrees.

Have I actually gotten better? Or do they only think so because of the disfraz? I gulp. Coco's friends almost never talk to me. I don't know what to say.

"So where's Coco?" Trish asks.

"She's out for a walk with our brother," I reply.

Trish steps back to make room for me on the sidewalk. "We're practicing our pop shove-its," she says. "Want to try?"

Trish jumps onto her board and rolls toward the curb. When she gets to the edge, she steps down on the tail of the skateboard, popping up the nose as she hops over. The board rotates front to back before she lands on top of it again.

"Your turn," Albert says.

I back up. I might look like an expert skater, but I'm really not.

"Come on, Cat," Trish says. "Let's see what you can do."

There might be *one* trick I can show them, something Coco has been teaching me. It's not as exciting as Trish's, but it's a small step. Like what Tía Abuela said.

I turn my skateboard wheels-up on the sidewalk and slide my feet underneath it. Then, as I jump, I flick the skateboard over with my toes and stomp on top of it, right side up.

"Nice!" Trish says.

Albert holds up his hand for a high five.

If the magic flannel works on the judges the same way it seems to be working on Trish and Albert, I just might win after all!

The rattling of wagon wheels interrupts my daydream. Uh-oh. I turn around.

"You were supposed to be fixing that shirt for *me*," Coco shouts. "Why is there a *cat* on it?"

· CHAPTER 8 ·

Sew Disappointing

*B*uenas tardes!" Papi calls out when Coco and I get home from school. She brushes by me without a word.

I step through the door and kick off my shoes. "Buenas tardes," I reply. But nothing feels very good about this afternoon.

Even though it's been more than a week, Coco still isn't speaking to me. It isn't *just* that I sewed that cat-shaped patch onto her flannel (although, she's pretty annoyed about that, too). It's that when she tried to put the shirt on again, it wouldn't fit over her shoulders. It must have shrunk in the wash!

"A package arrived for you," Papi says.

"It did?" I had almost given up hope. All of a sudden, the afternoon is looking *much* better. I run upstairs, hang up my backpack on its special peg in my room, and race back down to find Papi.

"Where is it?" I ask, panting. "The package?"

Before he can answer, I begin rummaging through the pile of mail he has stacked on the kitchen counter. I don't even bother to keep things in order the way I normally do.

Papi chuckles. "You must be expecting something pretty important."

Pretty important? That's an understatement.

"Only the *most* important thing I can think of," I tell Papi.

That's because the Dragon Dress 2.0 is not coming out the way I hoped it would. The silky green fabric I'm using is so slippery that I can't cut it in a straight line. Nothing is quite the right size even though I measured *three* times. Measuring is usually one of my specialties.

But just like me, Tía Abuela always has impeccable timing. If that package is from her, it couldn't have arrived at a more perfect moment. The Sewing Showcase opens this weekend. I'm sure she has sent me exactly what I need to save my dress.

"I set the package aside for you on the coffee table," Papi said. "I had a feeling you would be excited to open it."

I spin around on my heel and head straight for the living room. There's a brown envelope, right where Papi said it would be. And, just like I'd hoped, the stamp on the front says it came from

Belize. Even Tía Abuela's handwriting looks magical, with loopy letters written in shiny gold ink.

But the envelope is smaller than I was expecting. Part of me wished Tía Abuela would send me a finished dress. She probably thought that would be cheating, though. I shake the envelope. Maybe there are new sewing tools inside. Or a new spool of magical thread.

Carlos comes crawling in from the kitchen. "Mine?" he says, reaching for the envelope. I pull it away. *Whatever's* inside, I can't have his sticky hands all over it.

Finally I tear open the envelope, turn it upside down, and shake it out. A note flutters onto the coffee table, but I don't bother reading it yet. I'm too busy finding what else is in the envelope.

It's a surprise, all right. A big one. But not the good kind.

What I pull from the envelope is nothing like what I thought it might be. It's a scrap of fabric, with a line of messy, uneven stitches on it. They are so loose and crooked that it takes me several seconds to realize the stitches are *mine*. This is the piece of fabric Tía Abuela gave me to practice on when she taught me the running stitch for the first time.

They are the *opposite* of perfectly put together.

There must be some mistake, I think. Tía Abuela's surprise was supposed to *help* me with my showcase project. All this does is make me think about how terrible I used to be when I first started sewing.

I don't remember Tía Abuela's note until I notice

Carlos pulling himself up on the edge of the coffee table and grabbing it. I snatch it back from him a moment before he puts it into his mouth.

I unfold the thin piece of pink paper. It smells like oranges—one of Tía Abuela's favorite scents. No wonder Carlos thought it was a snack.

Querida Catalina, the note begins. *This is probably not the gift you were expecting.*

Not even close.

But before you get disappointed [too late for that!], *remember that the sewing kit was not what you expected either. In the end, it was more special than you realized.*

I keep reading.

Even if your dress doesn't turn out the way you imagined, you should be proud of how far you've come. I know I am! I hope these stitches remind you of where you started and inspire you to go even further.

I look down at the stitches again. The only thing they inspire me to do is hide them. I stuff the piece of fabric into my pocket.

At least it's Monday. That means there's a Stitch and Share session. If Tía Abuela won't help me with my showcase dress, I know the other sewists will.

· CHAPTER 9 ·

WORN AND TORN

*E*ven though I still feel bad that it doesn't fit Coco anymore, I plan to wear the flannel to Stitch and Share. I tell myself it's because I want to show Josefina and the other sewists my mending work. That's partly true, but it's not the only reason. I also want the burst of confidence I feel when I wear the shirt.

I need all the confidence I can get if I'm going to finish my gown. Especially now that Tía Abuela's surprise turned out to be such a flop. I'm starting to get nervous that I'm not as prepared to sew the Dragon Dress 2.0 as I thought I was.

I fold the silky green fabric pieces and pack them into my sewing bag, along with all my supplies. Since I know it's going to take a lot of work to finish the dress, I arrive at the library even earlier than usual. The community room is still empty, and the lights are off. I switch them on and spread the pieces of my dress out in the middle of the floor to examine them.

It's even worse than I thought.

I managed to sew the sleeves, but one is longer than the other. The bottom of the skirt is all crooked. The edges are beginning to fray.

"Catalina?"

"Aah!" I jump up, startled. But when I turn around to see who's there, it's only Josefina the

Librarian. She's carrying the fabric bin, and it's even emptier than it was last time.

"You're here early," Josefina continues. "Even for you." She looks down at my green fabric pieces. "What's all this?"

Now that my breath has slowed down, I kneel on the floor again. I explain my plan to recreate Tía Abuela's Dragon Dress in a size that would fit me.

"I bet lots of people would come to see it, and that would help you raise money for the sewing machine," I say. "I wanted to surprise you and the other sewists with the finished dress, but I'm having a little trouble." I frown. Even with all my practice, I can't seem to sew this dress.

Josefina sets the bin down on the desk at the back of the room. She comes back and sits on the floor next to me.

"You designed the dress yourself?" she asks.

I open my sewing bag and take out the notebook. I flip the pages until I get to the sketch I made of the dress, the one I showed Tía Abuela earlier.

Josefina takes the notebook and peers down at my drawing. Her glasses slide down her nose. Does she see something wrong with it?

"Hmm," Josefina says. "It takes a lot of creativity to design a dress like this. You have great attention to detail. Look at the sparkles on that collar!"

I take the notebook back. I already knew I have great attention to detail. That's why Tía Abuela trusted me with the sewing kit. But somehow the dress still turned into a major mess.

Josefina picks up one of the sleeves. "And you made the pattern on your own?"

I nod. "I didn't have a pattern, so I traced around one of the dresses I already had."

Josefina claps. "Good thinking!" she says. "Sometimes sewists have to be problem solvers. You have excellent problem-solving instincts."

But if I'm such an excellent problem solver, why is my dress in pieces?

Josefina puts the fabric down. She squeezes my shoulder. "This was a very *ambitious* project," she says. "That means you took on a big challenge, something much more difficult than anything you've ever sewn before. You should be proud."

I look down at the pile of green fabric on the floor and wrinkle my nose. "Proud of *that*?"

"Por supuesto," Josefina says. Of course. "And you should keep at it. If you try again next year, I bet you'll get even further."

Next year? "But I need to finish by Saturday!" I protest. "Otherwise I won't have a project to display in the Sewing Showcase!"

If Josefina can't help me, then none of the other sewists will be able to either.

I drop my head to my chest and fiddle with one of the new buttons I sewed on to Coco's flannel. It doesn't budge. My stitches are good and strong. Still, the shirt doesn't give me the burst of confidence that it did before.

"That's not Coco's old shirt, is it?" Josefina asks. "I almost didn't recognize it." She points to the patch on my elbow. "I love how you repaired that hole." I am not surprised. Josefina is a cat lover. Even her watch has a cat on it. The hour and minute hands are whiskers.

I look up, and when I do, Josefina notices the orange stitches on the pocket.

"Just look at that backstitch!" she exclaims. "I can see you've been practicing."

I can't hold back a smile, even though I'm still pretty disappointed.

"You know," Josefina goes on, "one of the most special things about knowing how to sew is being able to fix what's worn and torn. Why not use this shirt as your showcase project? People would learn a lot from it."

I shrug. "I'll think about it," I mumble. My eyes begin to sting. I pack up my fabric and all my supplies. For the first time since I started sewing, I *don't* stay for Stitch and Share.

CHAPTER 10

ＳMALL ＳTEPS

$\mathcal{E}$verything is falling apart, even worse than Coco's flannel was before I fixed it. I haven't helped my sister find her confidence again—I've only made her more upset.

As if that's not bad enough, I still don't have a project for the showcase. And now there isn't enough time, or enough fabric, to try again. Not even the magic sewing kit will help.

I stop in front of a trash bin on my way home and

lift the lid. I want to throw away the Dragon Dress—more like Dragon *Disaster*—so I never have to look at it again. But when I take one of the sleeves out of my sewing bag, I notice my stitches. I didn't realize before how straight and even they are.

I drop the trash can lid and dig into my pocket for the fabric scrap Tía Abuela sent. I compare my first stitches to my latest. They are so different that I almost can't believe I sewed both of them. This must be what Tía Abuela meant by taking small steps. I couldn't see how those small steps had added up—how far I've come—until I remembered where I'd started.

For the first time, I begin to feel a little better about the Dragon Dress 2.0. *And* about my sewing. Josefina is right. By next year, I'll make even more progress. I can't wait to see what my stitches look like then.

I jog the rest of the way home, in a hurry to talk

to Coco. Maybe if I remind her how far she's come too, she won't be so frustrated about all the trouble she's been having lately. Maybe she'll get some of that old Coco confidence back.

Only, she isn't outside practicing when I get home. Her skateboard is leaning against the side of the garage where I left it the other day. I sit down next to it and wriggle out of the flannel.

I could try to give it back to Coco. If I snip off the cat-shaped patch, it might feel like hers again. But she still won't be able to wear it. It doesn't fit anymore. Anyway, what will happen when it gets so worn-out that even I can't fix it?

Coco needs something that will last, that she can't ever outgrow. That she can carry around with her like the line of stitches I'm carrying in my pocket.

That's when I get another idea. My best one yet. Even better than the Dragon Dress 2.0.

I pull the cookie-tin sewing kit out of my bag and fish around inside for the scissors. It would be easier (not to mention tidier) to do this upstairs at my desk. But Coco might be there, and I want to surprise her.

I hold the shirt in one hand and the scissors in the other. I hesitate. If I go through with this, I won't be able to use the flannel as my Sewing Showcase project, even if I want to.

I also won't be able to wear it as a disfraz to impress the judges at the Skate Spectacular.

But Coco will.

I make the first cut.

· CHAPTER 11 ·

A Perfect Fit

It's the morning of the Skate Spectacular. I am pacing outside my bedroom with my sewing bag slung across my chest. My palms start to sweat, and *I'm* not even the one who is going to be late.

In fact, I woke up a whole hour earlier than usual to make sure I'd have enough time to get ready. When the alarm went off, I let it *brrrring* for two whole minutes, hoping it would wake Coco up too.

It didn't. She rolled right over and kept on

snoring. Coco could sleep through anything.

Including the Skate Spectacular if she doesn't wake up soon! I check my watch. Coco has exactly twenty-nine minutes to roll out of bed, get dressed, eat breakfast, and make it to the skate park in time for the competition.

Mami and Papi told me not to bother Coco. They said she needs her rest. But she'll never make it on time unless I do something. I wish I could put on the bumblebee disfraz. If I were incognito, I could buzz into the room and sting Coco out of bed without Mami and Papi even knowing.

I look down at my watch again. Twenty-*eight* minutes. That's it. I look right down the hall, then left toward the stairs, to make sure Mami and Papi aren't watching. When I'm sure they're not, I tiptoe into my room and grab a pillow off my bed.

With the pillow tucked under one arm, I climb

the ladder to the top bunk. I lift the pillow over my head to clobber Coco with it. But before I can bring it down, Coco raises herself up on an elbow and pulls out one of her earbuds.

"What are you doing?" she asks.

I let the pillow fall, sort of disappointed that I didn't get to use it. "You're awake," I say.

"Of course I'm awake. It's almost ten o'clock," Coco replies, as if she is *always* up at this time.

She is not.

"Then why are you still in bed?" I ask. If I had to sleep in Coco's bed, I'd jump out of it as soon as I could every morning. It's full of stray socks and who knows what else. "You should be getting ready for the Skate Spectacular. It's going to start without you."

Coco flops back down onto her pillow.

"Doesn't matter," she says. "I'm not going."

I had a feeling she might say that. After all, she hasn't been practicing all week.

As usual, I am prepared.

I sit at the edge of Coco's bed. I try not to think about how long it's been since she washed the sheets.

"But you've worked so hard," I tell her. "Don't you want to show everyone what you can do?"

Coco groans. "I still can't land the Coco-kick," she says. "And now that my lucky flannel doesn't fit anymore, I might never do it again."

This is the perfect moment. I reach into my sewing bag and take out Coco's flannel. What's left of it anyway.

"What if you could have your flannel back?" I ask, waving the cloth in front of her.

Coco sits straight up. She frowns. "What did you do to it?"

Uh-oh. Maybe I should have asked first.

The other day, leaning against the garage, I cut a big square out of the back of the shirt. That's the section that was the least faded and the least worn-out. I folded the square in half diagonally and turned it into a triangle. Then I sewed the two loose edges together with my strongest and neatest stitches.

"I turned it into a bandana!" I announce. "Now you'll never outgrow it. You'll always be able to keep it with you as a reminder of where you started. So what if you don't land the Coco-kick today? You've still come so far, one step at a time."

Coco snatches the bandana from my hands and stares at it. Our room is so quiet, I can hear the ticking of my watch. With each second that passes, I have to bite the inside of my cheek a little harder to stop myself from telling Coco to HURRY.

"I fell a lot before I landed that first trick," she

says finally. "But I stuck with it. Maybe that's what I need to do now."

She ties the bandana around her neck. It's a *perfect* fit. Thanks to my attention to detail.

"Does this mean you're going to skate in the competition?" I ask.

"If you ever get out of the way," she answers. "You're blocking the ladder."

I scramble down and check my watch. I gasp. "You only have twenty-one minutes to get there!"

Coco jumps down from the second-to-last wrung. Her confidence is already starting to come back, I can tell.

"*I* only have twenty-one minutes?" she says. "Aren't you coming too?"

Even though it's almost time for the Sewing Showcase, I can't miss Coco's comeback. Mami and

Papi and I pack Carlos into his wagon and race after her toward the park.

She's the last skater to arrive.

"You made it," says the woman at the check-in station.

"Right on time," Coco says with a grin.

"Hardly," I mutter. But I'm smiling too.

We find a spot to sit on the grass while Coco joins the other skaters. When her name is announced, I watch Coco push off and glide down a ramp. It's not the fastest I've ever seen her, but at least she doesn't jump off this time.

Coco zigzags around the park, then hops up onto a rail. So far, so good.

Mami whistles. Papi and Carlos clap.

I'm too nervous to join them—it's nearly time for the Coco-kick.

Coco builds up speed. She steps down hard on

the back of the board and rockets upward. But she doesn't get high enough for the board to spin all the way around before she comes down again. She lands crooked, with one foot on the ground.

Oh no. I twirl a curl tight around my finger, worried that Coco will be disappointed.

But after she yanks her helmet off, she pumps her fist in the air and shouts, "I'm back!"

Finally I can cheer. Even if she doesn't win the competition, Coco has beaten her skateboard slump. That's a big step.

I start to race down the hill to congratulate her.

"Shouldn't you get to the library?" Papi asks. "You're going to be late."

Impossible. I'm never late. I look down at my watch. The Sewing Showcase opens in five minutes!

"See you later, Kitty-Cat!" Mami yells. I'm already racing to the library.

· CHAPTER 12 ·

A New Journey

Pablo Blanco is already standing at the library entrance when I arrive. I frown. I was hoping I could still get here before him.

He's tapping his foot as if he has been waiting outside for *hours* instead of only a few minutes.

"It's about time you got here," he says. "The showcase opened four minutes and forty-seven seconds ago."

On the outside, I roll my eyes. But inside I'm

happy that Pablo is here. Even if he *is* being a little persnickety. I'm still nervous about my showcase display, and it feels better having a friend here with me.

"Well, let's not stand here wasting even more time," I say. "Let's go inside."

Pablo sniffs in reply. He puts his nose in the air and walks into the building. I march in behind him.

Everything is all set up in the community room. I realize I'm even more excited to see the other sewists' projects than I am to show off my own. But first we stop at the donation jar that Josefina has set on a table near the entrance. Each of us drops some coins inside.

I try to count up the money in the jar and wonder if it's enough to buy a sewing machine. But before I'm finished, Pablo grabs my wrist.

"Are those puppies?" He yanks me over to Anthony Becerra's project. "You never said there were puppies at Stitch and Share."

Usually there aren't. Josefina the Librarian gave Anthony special permission to bring some dogs from the animal shelter to the showcase opening. They're playing inside a small pen. One gnaws on a purple chew toy.

"I made that!" I tell Pablo. It's one of the toys we helped Anthony make for the animal shelter.

Nearby, two puppies nap on one of Anthony's pet beds. "They look very comfortable," I say.

"Gracias!" Anthony replies. He can't talk long.

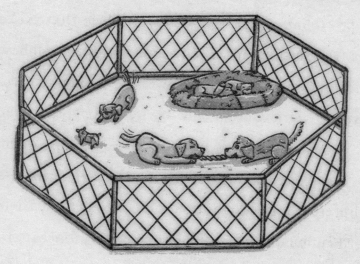

Someone is waiting to order a handmade pet bed from him!

Pablo leans in close and whispers, "Did he really make that himself?"

I nod.

I expect him to say it reminds him of something he once saw in a telenovela, but he doesn't. Instead he whistles. "Maybe I should learn to sew too."

And maybe *I've* just recruited Stitch and Share's newest member.

We admire the tiny pieces of fabric that make up Mrs. Glass's quilt. Both Pablo and I can tell how much attention to detail it must have taken to carefully cut and sew each one.

Next we check out the collection of puppets Ms. Yoo sewed, and Mr. Hart's finished cap. He even lets Pablo try it on.

Then, when we see Señora Garcia's quinceañera

gown, with its shimmering satin and piles of fluffy tulle, Pablo gasps. "This is even better than the costumes on the new show Mom and I are watching!"

Josefina the Librarian chuckles as she walks up to us. "Catalina! Pablo!" she says. "I see you're enjoying the showcase."

I point to the donation jar. It's filling fast. "Looks like you'll have enough to buy lots of new supplies for Stitch and Share," I say.

Josefina grins. "That means lots more practice for you," she agrees. "Have you shown Pablo *your* project yet?"

I was saving it for last.

I lead Pablo to the table where my display is set up.

"Did you finish the Dragon Dress two-point-oh?" he asks, walking a little faster. Tía Abuela happens to be Pablo's favorite actor. He was probably looking forward to seeing my replica of her gown.

"Not exactly," I admit. "I need more time to get it right. So I came up with something different. What do you think?"

I emptied my craft bin—and used every single one of my colored pencils—to make a poster board that shows my sewing progress so far.

Pinned on one side is the fabric scrap Tía Abuela sent, the one with my very first stitches. On the rest of the board, I've displayed examples of the projects I've worked on in Stitch and Share: one of the dozens of pillowcases Josefina made me sew, a drawstring pouch, the vest I made to wear in the talent show, and even the butterfly wings that were part of a magical disfraz. (I hope no one notices the silvery thread that sparkles a little more brightly than it should.)

At the top of the poster board I've written "My Sewing Journey."

Pablo's eyes widen. He presses his lips together.

I can tell he's trying hard not to smile. He squints. "Pretty good," he says. "But I bet I could sew even neater stitches."

I laugh. "You could try, but you'd better start practicing."

Just then I hear the familiar whir of rolling wheels. I snap my head around. It's Coco! She's still wearing her lucky bandana.

I'm about to tell her that she shouldn't be riding her skateboard inside the library. It's against the rules. But then I look down and notice she's not riding her skateboard. She's riding a new one.

"You won?"

Coco leaps off the board and pops it up into her arms. "I won! I didn't land the Coco-kick perfectly, but no one else even attempted it."

Pablo frowns and scoots away, but I throw my arms around Coco's neck and hug her.

"Let's go celebrate at the skate park," she says. "Your new board is parked right outside. I even brought your helmet."

My new board? I can't wait. I turn to Pablo. "Want to come?"

He shakes his head. "I think I'm going to stay and take another look at that hat," he says. "I might want to make one myself."

I'm sure he can do it. Someday.

"Don't forget," I call over my shoulder as I follow Coco out the door. "It's going to be a long journey. Just take it one small step at a time."

Turn the page for a
sneak peek at Catalina's
first magical adventure!

BY JENNIFER TORRES

CATALINA
INCOGNITO

ILLUSTRATED BY
GLADYS JOSE

ATTENTION TO DETAIL

The picture on the puzzle box shows three gray kittens peeking out of a picnic basket.

Kittens. Of *course*.

If Mami and Papi didn't give me a kitten puzzle for my birthday, they would give me a kitten sticker collection. And if they didn't give me a kitten sticker collection, they would give me a kitten coloring book. Even though they know I am getting too old for all this kitten stuff. And even though I have told them to quit calling me "Kitty-Cat" and start using my real name, Catalina.

Everyone in my family—Mami and Papi; Baby Carlos in his high chair; my big sister, Coco; and Tía Abuela—is sitting around the kitchen table. They all lean forward, watching me.

"Well, Kitty-Cat," Papi asks, "what do you think?"

The first thing I think is, *Quit calling me "Kitty-Cat."*

But that's not what I say, because the *second* thing I think is that even though I don't love kittens as much as I used to, I still love puzzles. You get to figure out exactly where each piece belongs, and when you're finished, you know you haven't made any mistakes.

"It's perfect," I say.

"Maybe we can work on it together," Mami suggests.

Carlos claps. A droplet of drool drips off his lip and onto the high chair tray. I picture it landing on my puzzle. I fold my arms over the box to protect it from even the *idea* of Carlos's baby slobber.

"Hmm," I reply. Not quite a yes, and not exactly a no.

Luckily, Coco slides her gift across the table before I have to give a real answer.

She has wrapped it in this morning's newspaper. And lots and lots of tape. I don't have to open it to know what's inside—her old skateboard helmet.

"I'll even let you borrow my board," Coco says. She pulls the brim of her baseball cap lower down on her forehead. It hides her eyes, but not her smirk. "Unless you're still too scared after what happened the first time."

"I am *not* scared," I say, but my cheeks go warm

as I remember last summer's wipeout.

Papi slaps his hands on the table. "Bravo, Coco!" he says. "Did you hear that, Kitty-Cat? Your sister is going to teach you to skateboard."

I don't need Coco to teach me, I think. This year I am ready. This year I will be perfect.

"Thank you, *Consuelo*," I say. I make my voice as sweet as a sip of horchata on a sunny afternoon. "You are *too* generous."

At last it is time to open Tía Abuela's gift. Tía Abuela's gifts are always the best.

Tía Abuela is Papi's aunt—my great-aunt—and her name is Catalina Castañeda too.

Only, most people know her as "La Chispa," the spark, one of the rottenest villains in telenovela history. Before she retired, the characters she played on TV were awfully, monstrously, fabulously *bad*. The rich but cruel stepmother. The beautiful but wicked duchess. The evil twin. Fans say her acting was so amazing, it was as if she *transformed* into every character.

Tía Abuela doesn't visit our house on the hill in Valle Grande very often. She's too busy traveling the world. But she always sends souvenirs home to my brother and sister and me.

Tía Abuela is only in town for the grand opening of the Catalina Castañeda Children's Room at the Valle Grande Central Library. The library was her favorite place to visit when she was growing up. It's where she first learned all about heroes and villains and adventures.

She's also here to celebrate my birthday, of course.

She has just returned from exploring the ancient Mayan city of Palenque in Mexico. Her gift comes in a box, wrapped in shimmering gold paper and a purple ribbon. I try to imagine what's inside. "An archaeologist's hand shovel?" I guess. "Ooh! I know, a map of the jungle!"

But when I untie the ribbon, tear apart the paper, and open the box, I don't find either of those things.

What I find instead is a red velvet pouch. It isn't new. Not even *almost* new. In fact, the pouch is so ancient, the cloth is worn bald in places.

It reminds me a little of an old dog with patchy fur. I try not to wrinkle my nose.

I know I should smile.

I know I should say "Thank you."

I know I should say *something*.

But I worry that if I so much as twitch, the groan I am trying to swallow will come tumbling out of my mouth before I can stop it.

"Not what you were expecting?" Tía Abuela says with a snort.

Not even close.

But it would be rude to just say so. So I don't.

I open the pouch and peer inside. There is a little brass thimble, a spool of silver thread, and a needle poking out of a strawberry-shaped pincushion.

Nope. Definitely not what I was expecting.

"Cata*lina* . . ." Mami nudges me with her voice. It's my name, but it is also a warning.

I try to think of something polite to say. "Thank you, Tía Abuela. It is so . . . so . . . so *different*."

Tía Abuela cackles. "Do you even know what it is, Kitty-Cat?"

I shake my head.

"It is a sewing kit. I've had it since I was your age. I thought it was the perfect gift for someone with your . . . How shall I put this?" She pauses. She taps a flamingo-pink fingernail against her lips as she thinks of the right thing to say. "Someone with your *attention to detail*. Attention to detail is very important when it comes to sewing."

"Hmm" is all I say.